Proximity Publishing
700 W. Pete Rose Way
Cincinnati, OH 45203

Library of Congress Control Number: 2011933091
ISBN 978-0615504-834

Printed in China

alcott afoot

Written by
Steve Kissing

Illustrated by
David Schlosser

Based on a story by
Troy Hitch

"I have never been one to take chances, Alcott,"
said Elsa. "And I believe that I've lived to regret it.
I should very much like to go on an adventure now."

Alcott didn't know what regret meant, but adventure,
well, that sounded like fun.

"Isn't this so exciting, Alcott?" Elsa said. "We will soon be world travelers, going farther than we ever have."

Alcott was pleased to see Elsa so thrilled. And he wondered about all the new things he would see.

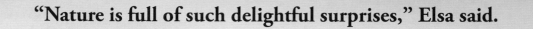

"Nature is full of such delightful surprises," Elsa said.

Alcott noticed another surprise: he was standing beyond Elsa's shadow. That hadn't happened much. It felt good. He leapt toward the sky, just like the geyser.

OLD FAITHFUL GEYSER

"So many people in the world, Alcott, and each one deliciously different," said Elsa.

Alcott couldn't agree more, and he was glad to be making new friends. Especially one as pretty as Monique.

"You keep howling like that, Alcott, and they might put you in tonight's performance," said Elsa.

Alcott was beginning to believe he could do just about anything.

"It's hard not to feel small looking at these majestic mountains," said Elsa.

This made Alcott smile because the tiny bug he watched made him feel so big.

"This was built as a sign of eternal love," said Elsa. "Think of me whenever you see it again in pictures. Or perhaps on a return visit."

Alcott was busy enjoying the interesting smells of a nearby vendor, but Elsa's comment caught his attention.

"I feel like I'm looking in a mirror, Alcott," said Elsa.
"I've been leaning for some time, too."

For the first time, Alcott noticed that Elsa looked a little old.
And lonely. He began to wonder if maybe, just maybe, he had
been too focused on himself and his own adventures.

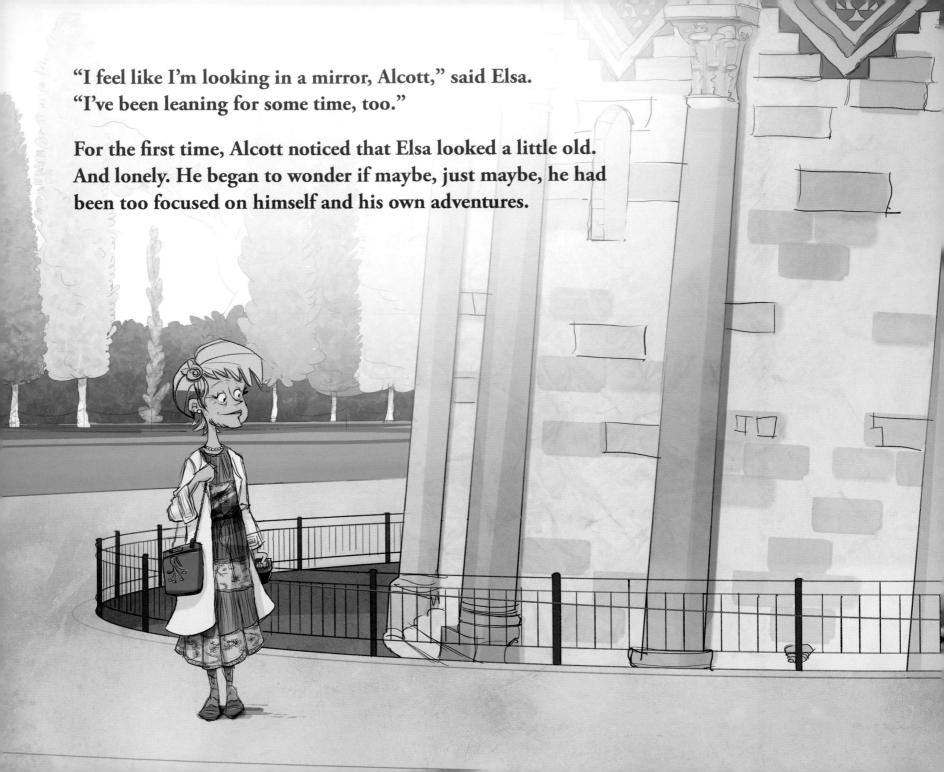

"Alcott, these kites make my heart sing," said Elsa.

They made Alcott feel good, too. And he was taken by how the kites' owners were as proud of their kites when they rested in their arms as when they danced in the sky. This got Alcott to thinking.

"Alcott, have you ever seen such beauty?" asked Elsa. "The flowers make my eyes feel young again."

Inspired by the windmills, Alcott rolled over twice, moving closer to Elsa. And that made him feel warm inside. Elsa, too.

"My dear Alcott, to hear Beethoven in Vienna is such sweet perfection!" said Elsa. "It's enough to make me cry."

Alcott turned around to be sure that any tears were happy tears. They were.

"In all my years, I've never seen monkeys in the wild," said Elsa. "How playful they are!"

This was new for Alcott, too. He thought about how much of the jungle the babies got to see while clinging tightly to their mothers.

"A long, long time ago, the Mayans
built these wonderful playgrounds," said Elsa.
"If I had something to toss, we could play fetch."

Truth be told, Alcott was glad Elsa didn't have a stick.
He enjoyed being nearby.

"You need not worry, Alcott," said Elsa. "We're quite safe here. Besides, I'd never let any harm come to you."

Alcott had seen the world, but he sensed that though he was closer to home and closer to Elsa, he was still seeing some special things.

"Alcott, what a wonderful trip we had!" said Elsa.
"But, I must say: It feels good to be home."

Alcott felt the exact same way. Adventures come in
all shapes and sizes, he thought. And they happen
near and far. He wondered what adventure was next.